MW00762546

The Adventures of Edward - The Baby Liraffe

Written by Jack Le Raff

Illustrated by Casie Trace

Book Design by Carie Pace

www.liraffe.com

First edition published and printed in Bermuda 2017
A copy of this book has been deposited in the Bermuda National Library
Copyright © 2017
ISBN #: 978-0-947480-37-0

To AryA,
BEST WISHES,
Jxem.

Far, far away in a land of orange sky lived a loveable Lion called George and his beautiful wife Joy, a gentle and graceful Giraffe. This African land was known as Freeland, home to all types of exotic wildlife and splendid animals.

George and Joy lived happily near a tranquil place called Lake Blue. George would spend his days drinking and swimming in the luscious water, before a long sleep under an umbrella tree. Joy usually spent her time eating the scrumptious acacia leaves from the tall trees and visiting their animal friends close by.

Most days followed the same routine, peaceful and quiet, until one very special day!
Joy had been carrying a large bump in her tummy and on this magical day she gave birth to a
little baby boy. Joy and George could not have been happier.

After a few days of nursing and caring for the little one, George called on all their lake
friends for a great celebration to meet the newest and smallest member of their family.

That night around a blazing fire in a grass clearing, all George and Joy's friends gathered together. There were Bru and Leigh the monkeys, with their own special newborn - Thomas; Lugsy the elephant, Olive the rhino, Henry the hippo and his wife Jess, Florence the flamingo, Willy the wildebeest and many others, all anxious to have even the smallest glimpse of the new baby arrival.

At the edge of the clearing, contently lying in a comfy bed of African violet leaves, lay a tiny baby 'Liraffe' (now, if you don't know what a Liraffe is, well it is half a lion, and half a giraffe)."Everybody" announced Joy excitedly, "this is little baby Edward!"

The animals gasped and huddled in closer for a better look. "He's one of the 'smiliest' animals I've ever seen!" squeaked Leigh. Edward gave a small baby giggle and started to chew on his bed leaves. "He has your appetite George!" Lugsy chuckled.

And the gathering laughed as Edward ate nearly all of his bed from underneath him. It was at that moment that George and Joy saw for the first time that Edward loved eating leaves more than anything! The celebrations continued long into the night with laughter and storytelling under the inky blue sky until the sun rose sleepily from the dawn.

At early daybreak all of the animals slowly trundled home,
marvelling still at the newborn baby in their midst.

Over the following months, baby Edward learned to walk and explore the grasslands near his home.

Most days he would happily spend the mornings with Joy eating leaves in the shade or paddling and splashing in the lake to cool himself down from the hot African sun.

In the afternoons, he would be
skipping around with his friends
or with George, snoozing
under the shelter of the umbrella trees.

Although Edward was growing and learning to walk and talk, he stayed very small and his neck and legs did not grow long like his mothers. And so, each day, his mum helped feed him by stretching her long neck to pick the leaves from the tall trees and bring them down for Edward to eat.

Edward's favourite thing in all the world was to eat green leaves. Acacia, Mimosa, shoots and herbs, it didn't matter to Edward – he would eat them all! Always with a big smile on his face.

Edward had many friends in the grasslands but he spent most of his time with Thomas, the young baby monkey. Thomas and Edward loved exploring far and wide around the lake, discovering new canyons and creeks to play in, seeing all new landscapes - visiting places they had not seen before, and they could never sit still!

As Thomas was a monkey, he would climb the trees and drop down leaves from the branches for Edward whenever he was hungry. He really was a very happy little Liraffe.

One day, when Edward was down at the lake, he spotted something strange on the shore flapping in the light breeze. It was a travel magazine that had been forgotten by a wandering tourist.

Edward had never seen anything like it. As he turned the pages with his snout he saw pictures of incredible scenes he couldn't believe. Far away places with rivers and waterfalls, mountains and glaciers, cities and oceans. It was a whole new world and much, much bigger than Lake Blue.

For a long while Edward could not stop thinking about the new world he had seen in the magazine. At feeding one night he couldn't contain his excitement anymore and told his mum and dad of all the wonderful places he had learned about and how he wished to set off and explore them all.

This came as a big surprise to his mum and dad and later that evening when Edward was asleep George and Joy sat around the fire and discussed the possibility of Edward travelling overseas.

Although they both would be sad for him to go, they also knew it was time for Edward to leave the lake and discover the wonders of the big wide world for himself.

So George and Joy called a meeting with Bru, Leigh, Henry, Jess and the older members of Lake Blue to think of ways to help Edward on his travels.

Willy provided a red backpack that he had found abandoned by campers by the lake; Bru brought a map of Africa that he had snaffled from a safari jeep; Henry and Jess provided clean drinking water; and Thomas gave the best treasure of all - a shiny bronze compass.

Joy made sure that any room left in the backpack was stuffed with his favourite acacia leaves to keep him happy and full of energy on his journey.

Lugsy the elephant, the most travelled of the group, had spoken to the local safari camp who had kindly agreed that Edward could travel with a safari ranger by jeep to Kenya where she was due to tend to some sick animals.

The following few days Edward was beside himself with excitement about his upcoming travels. On his fifth birthday the inhabitants of Lake Blue held a huge party to celebrate his big departure the very next day. There were animals as far as the eye could see.

Around the crackling beach fire the monkeys juggled pineapples, the elephants displayed a waterfight, the hippos and the wildebeest sang songs, while Edward and his family sat by the beach and watched and laughed.

The next sunrise, Edward, all packed with his bursting backpack, sniffed farewell to his mum and dad before boarding the back of the safari jeep. Joy cried with her long neck bowed, while George passed on his wise words to be a good little Liraffe, make friends, respect others, but be careful and stay out of trouble!

And with that, the jeep sped off onto the dusty track, taking Edward away on his adventures. He waved and waved to his parents until he could see them no more and they were just tiny specs in the distance. Although he was sad to be leaving everyone at Lake Blue behind he was at the same time very excited for the big adventure ahead.

That day he and the ranger drove 400 kilometres along the bumpy trail until they approached their resting place just in time for sundown. Edward was very tired by now and was already dreaming of a long night's sleep under the shimmering stars.

But, as the jeep started to slow Edward began to hear an unfamiliar roaring sound in the distance getting louder and louder.

"What is that noise?!" he shouted to the front of the truck. Edward started to feel a bit scared and huddled down into a tiny ball in the back of the jeep as it finally came to a halt.

The noise now the engine had stopped was very loud indeed. The ranger came round to the back of the jeep and let down the ramp door, but Edward was not budging, and was trembling terribly from the deafening din.

"Come on now Edward, there's nothing to be afraid of" the ranger told him comfortingly. Still Edward didn't move, now covering his head with his front hooves. The ranger finally climbed on board and gently persuaded Edward to shuffle out of the truck corner and down onto the road.

"Welcome to Victoria Falls! This is the tallest waterfall in all of Africa!" exclaimed the ranger proudly. Edward didn't know what to think, he had never heard of a waterfall before. "Don't be scared, come with me" the ranger said laughing, waving him to walk along.

And with that the two edged closer to a viewing point right on the cusp of the gigantic drop. Edward's mouth dropped wide open as he gasped at this most beautiful sight, the water crashing over the cliffs and rainbow colours spilling out of the mist floating through the air.

That evening the driver started a camp fire some distance from the falls while Edward splashed and bathed in the 'Devil's Pool', washing off the dirt from the journey and feeling fresh again. Every few minutes when he was feeling brave Edward would paddle up to the edge and stare at the cascading water rushing past him and down into a seemingly endless abyss.

Under the dark night sky, the stars winking at each other in turn, the baby Liraffe sat warm around the fire listening to the young gamekeeper's stories of all the different types of animal he looked after at the Freeland Safari Reserve, Edward fascinated by this undiscovered world. As the night drew on they both packed-up wearily from the travel of the day, and laid out their rugs and settled down to sleep.

As fresh as daisies the two woke the next morning, having slept heavy by the fire, and breathing in the crisp air of the misty falls. After a cup of steaming hot coffee for the driver and a bowl of the freshest falls water for Edward, they climbed back into the jeep and headed north towards Kenya.

As they travelled, the sprawling African landscape unfurled in front of the young Liraffe. So happy was Edward to learn more of this vast continent he was proud to call home. Passing the majestic Kilimanjaro with its white capped summit he learned of snow, something that confused him greatly.

And having only heard of them from George's bedtime stories, Edward watched in awe as a full parade of elephants in the distance swept across the grassy savannah of Tanzania.

It was another long morning and afternoon drive before they neared the border of Kenya. The driver slowed the jeep and excitedly Edward jumped up alert with his front hooves on the cab roof thinking they had arrived at the next destination. "We're not there yet Edward," whispered the driver. "We've got to be quiet and sit still for a moment." Well this left Edward very puzzled indeed and he couldn't understand what they were waiting for.

Until…every so slowly Edward started to feel a rumbling moving from the prairie land beneath them and up through the jeep. Each second the rumbling increasing and a dull roar lifting from just over the brow ahead of them.

When the rumbling was at fever pitch suddenly hundreds and hundreds of gazelle, wildebeest and zebras thundered over the horizon directly towards them! "It's the Great Migration!" screamed the driver, finding it hard to shout over the noise. "Every year the animals charge south for calving in the short grasslands."

Edward stood mesmerised on the quaking jeep, shaking from side to side now as the wildebeest charged by, kicking up dust and bumping the vehicle as they passed. Apart from the sheer fear and exhilaration of the spectacle all around them, Edward was fascinated with the bounding gazelle, leaping high with their horns in the air, and grew curious of the striped zebra that he had never seen before. What a marvellous sight!

After what felt like hours, the herds had finally passed and the duo slowly continued off into Kenya, now covered head to hoof in dirt.

Night fell and they arrived finally at their destination, the fabulous Giraffe Manor. "Edward, this is where I have to leave you. You will find good company here till your next ride. I must go because I have to collect a sick rhino to take back to Freeland and tend to him," explained the ranger. "Oh no!" worried Edward, "I hope you make him well again! Thank you for everything, I won't forget the travels and everything you've shown me."

"You're welcome Edward" shouted the ranger as she jumped into the jeep and revved off down the track, kicking up a cloud of orange dust in her wake. Edward trotted back to the magnificent manor house, chatted briefly with its owners, and exhausted from the long day taking in all the astounding sights, settled into their spare stable for the evening.

Edward awoke the next morning to the sound of the early birds chirping - he sprung out of bed ready to explore this magnificent building and all its fine pointed walls, windows and trimmings - when suddenly he heard a curious voice talking from out of nowhere. "Oh gosh! What a cute little thing you are!" said the mysterious voice.

Edward looked around flummoxed until he peered straight up to see a giraffe poking her long neck round the corner of the building looking down at him. The tall and elegant female strutted around the corner with not one, not two, but three other majestic looking giraffes! Edward was so very excited to see familiar animals again.

The tower of giraffes stooped their heads low to take a closer look at baby Edward and say hello. Immediately the baby Liraffe felt welcomed and at home.

"I'm Nekki, this is my husband Hensi,
and these are our friends Kimbo and Ninki."

From behind Nekki, a delightful baby giraffe coyly stepped out into view.

"Hello, I'm Emily," she said, batting her eyelashes.
What a pretty little lady Edward thought!
"I'm Edward, nice to meet you all."

"We're pleased to meet you! Where are you from?" asked the mother giraffe.
"I'm from Lake Blue in Freeland" replied Edward excitedly.

As the group of giraffes inquisitively sniffed and nuzzled around him, Edward explained that he was half lion and half giraffe, and told of all his friends back home, of the lake, his days exploring with Thomas, and the terrific farewell party they had.

"I know your mother!" laughed Nekki.
Edward beamed a huge smile, larger than usual. "Really??" he burst.
"Yes, a long, long time ago. When we were young we used to gallop the 'Hot Hoof Relay Race' around Lake Croc. She was very fast your mother, and we used to win a lot of prizes!"

Edward sighed with pride and grinned with happy thoughts of the family back home.

That afternoon the giraffes and Edward hunkered down in a huddle on the grass and swapped stories of their adventures under the soothing warmth of the African sun.

When they grew peckish, they would tour the manor and poke their heads through the windows to say hello to the visiting guests. If they were lucky, some kindly folks would even pass them leaves and vegetables from their dinner plates!

Edward and Emily made friends very quickly. Emily normally doesn't see animals the same age as her so Edward was a welcome surprise.

To stretch their legs Emily and Edward would canter around the many buildings of the manor and the skirts of the outer paddock. The baby Liraffe had so much fun, always chuckling and giggling with happiness.

They played a lot of hide and seek which gave Edward a big advantage due to his small size; and 'catch-me-if-you-can' where Emily seemed to always get caught in the perimeter fencing, partly due to her being born with unusually large 'pom-pom' hooves which made her ever so clumsy!

Before packing up in the morning of his departure, Nekki trotted round to Edward's guest stable. "Edward – Hensi, Emily and I have been talking overnight. We thought it would be a good thing for Emily growing up if she could travel and see more of this world. Now that we've met you we know she has a friend to help look after her on her first travels........she can be a bit, you know....accident prone! Could she travel with you?"

Edward loved the idea of a companion on his journey. "That would be a lot of fun" he said beaming a big grin. "Great!" shrieked Nekki, "let me go and check with the driver if it is ok for one more passenger."

Edward had spent two glorious days at Giraffe Manor before it was time to move on with his journey. He thanked the owner and the giraffes for a wonderful time and promised Nekki that he would say hi to his mother for her when he returned back to Lake Blue and of course look after Emily.

He had made some great friends here and hoped to see them again soon.

For now though, he and Emily were bound for the Mediterranean Sea! It was arranged that a guide would take them in a Land Rover, across Ethiopia, and north through The Sudan and Egypt. There was more to see, and much more to amaze.

For two days and two nights they drove along the meandering River Nile until arriving in Egypt. Edward and Emily were about to see their first of the Seven Wonders of the World - well, if the main building at Giraffe Manor was a sight to behold, this was truly enormous!

Before them was the Sphynx and the Great Pyramid of Giza. As the driver explained the history of the Egyptian Pharoahs who had created these monumental sites, Edward and Emily, now tilted on back hooves staring upward, marvelled at how anyone could build such a thing – and at that moment both giraffe and Liraffe felt very, very small indeed!

Upon entering Cairo, the first city that they had ever seen, they found themselves joyfully entertained by all the wonderful white buildings, and the symmetry and logic of them, connected by streets and roads and alleyways. It was all very organized and confusing.

Edward struggled to comprehend why there was so little space and why the noisy Land Rover could not roam wherever it wished. Edward was so used to cantering around in any direction he pleased, and as free as a bird, meanwhile Emily was quite acquainted with structure, buildings and being penned-in.

At mid-afternoon they arrived in Cairo's centre and were dropped off by the guide where they parted and enthusiastically waved a thankful hoof goodbye. Keen to explore this brave new world, the four-legged wanderers followed their snouts to the Friday Market. They entered the bustling streets, choc-a-block with stalls and market-sellers, haggling over prices and the best deal.

Emily was particularly mesmerised and completely distracted by the gold, gemstones, fabrics and Egyptian cotton on display. Edward seemed much more captivated by the curious wafts of unfamiliar food in the air.

Trotting aimlessly through the market Emily was suddenly drawn towards a herb and spice stall. The stall had ground spices, all colours of the rainbow, and a variety of green herbs, and the mix of all their scents was starting to make Edward VERY VERY hungry.

"Edward, look at this!" she whinnied. "Have you ever seen such crazy exotic colours?!" With an untamed sense of curiousity Emily couldn't stop herself and nudged her snout up close for a big sniff.

Not knowing what she was in for, she bellowed out a huge sneeze, puffing up a giant cloud of rainbow powder!! Stunned by the mix of pastel and neon now plastered on their multi-coloured faces, they stood shellshocked in silence looking down at the now vastly empty spice buckets. Not to mention a very angry stallkeeper.

"Run!!" yelped Emily as she turned and bolted down the market way, galloping inbetween shoppers legs and toppling vases, amphoras and other such antiquities along the way. As Edward made out to follow he couldn't resist taking a big chomp out of the multiple green shades on the herb rack, infuriating the stallkeeper even further, before scampering after Emily.

For about twenty minutes or so they ran before tiring and reaching the northern border of the city where they could see the port, their last stop before leaving Africa.

They slowly wandered towards their destination giggling and laughing at the day's escapades, Edward oddly charmed by Emily's clumsiness and being every bit as accident prone as Nekki had warned him.

Finally they arrived at Port Sa'id on the mouth of the Nile delta where the river met the Mediterranean Sea. From here they would take a small craft transporting cotton across to the mainland of Europe.

Before long they were tucked up in the closed quarters of the ship amongst giant bales of cotton. Exhausted from the huge day of travel and the chaos at the market, Emily slumped down cozily against Edward and started to feel ever so sleepy. They were sure to have a quiet and peaceful night sleep here.

With dusk looming Edward and Emily felt the chug of the engines start and the vessel pull away from the port. Excitement took over and they both leapt up and galloped down the gangway to watch the departure.

Stood on their hind legs, front hooves on the railing they smiled their farewells to Egypt and the rest of Africa, promising to return soon. The boat drifted further out to sea, and the clanging and clattering of the busy port gradually started to fade, and as darkness fell the city lights began to twinkle bright against the deep night sky.

What a week it had been for the tiny Liraffe who had only known before a blue lake, mountains, grasslands and yummy, yummy acacia trees. Edward felt chuffed to bits to be exploring this exciting big wide world, experiencing new sights and sounds and making new friends like Emily. What fun this all is!

But there was so much more adventure to come…

...soon they would arrive in Europe!

———————————— o ————————————

CAIRO

GIRAFFE
MANOR

MOUNT
KILIMANJARO

VICTORIA
FALLS

FREELAND

N
W   E
S

AFRICA

Giraffe Manor - Nairobi, Kenya

Located on the outskirts of Nairobi, Kenya, and dating back to the 1930's, Giraffe Manor is one of East Africa's most iconic buildings. The hotel itself is home to a number of resident Rothchild giraffe who visit the Manor in the mornings and evenings to greet guests and sniff out some snacks before venturing out to their sanctuary.

Giraffe Manor's lifelong ambition is the preservation of this beautiful and threatened species, and in supporting that cause offers an unrivalled experience including breakfast with the giraffes, an exquisite dining experience, guided walks within the giraffe conservation, and a complimentary car service to take you to all the tourist attractions in the local area. For more information on Giraffe Manor please visit:

www.thesafaricollection.com.

The Elsa Conservation Trust

The Elsa Conservation Trust is a charity registered in the UK dedicated to conserving wildlife and protecting animal habitats in Kenya and East Africa. It was originally founded by George and Joy Adamson in the 1960's who fostered Elsa, an orphan lion cub, inspiring the 1966 film classic Born Free. This book celebrates the 50th anniversary of Born Free and George and Joy's life's work. More fully, the Trust's vision is to extend its programme to respond to the many emerging environmental challenges in Kenya today. Last year around 15,000 students and teachers passed through the Trust's centre of education for sustainability, benefitting both people and the environment.

The Trust is a valued institution in Kenya's wildlife community and a leading embassador for the protection of animals like Edward, Emily, and his pals. 10% of profits from this book are donated to the Trust's mission. If you would like to learn more about the Elsa Conservation Trust or make a contribution directly, please visit their website at www.elsatrust.org.